Good Sports

A Viking Easy-to-Read

by **Dori Chaconas**
illustrated by **Lisa McCue**

VIKING

VIKING
Published by Penguin Group
Penguin Young Readers Group,
345 Hudson Street, New York, New York 10014, U.S.A.
Penguin Group (Canada), 90 Eglinton Avenue East, Suite 700, Toronto,
Ontario, Canada M4P 2Y3 (a division of Pearson Penguin Canada Inc.)
Penguin Books Ltd, 80 Strand, London WC2R 0RL, England
Penguin Ireland, 25 St Stephen's Green, Dublin 2, Ireland (a division of Penguin Books Ltd)
Penguin Group (Australia), 250 Camberwell Road, Camberwell, Victoria 3124, Australia
(a division of Pearson Australia Group Pty Ltd)
Penguin Books India Pvt Ltd, 11 Community Centre, Panchsheel Park,
New Delhi - 110 017, India
Penguin Group (NZ), Cnr Airborne and Rosedale Roads, Albany,
Auckland 1310, New Zealand (a division of Pearson New Zealand Ltd)
Penguin Books (South Africa) (Pty) Ltd, 24 Sturdee Avenue, Rosebank,
Johannesburg 2196, South Africa

Penguin Books Ltd, Registered Offices: 80 Strand, London WC2R 0RL, England

Published in 2007 by Viking, a division of Penguin Young Readers Group

1 3 5 7 9 10 8 6 4 2

LIBRARY OF CONGRESS CATALOGING-IN-PUBLICATION DATA
Chaconas, Dori, date–
Cork and Fuzz : good sports / by Dori Chaconas ; illustrated by Lisa McCue.
p. cm.
Summary: Short-legged Cork is upset when tall Fuzz wins every game they play,
until he learns that their friendship is more important than winning.
ISBN 978-0-670-06145-7 (hardcover)
[1. Best friends—Fiction. 2. Competition (Psychology)—Fiction. 3. Opossums—Fiction.
4. Muskrat—Fiction. 5. Friendship—Fiction.] I. McCue, Lisa, ill. II. Title.
PZ7.C342Cog 2007
[E]—dc22
2006001344

Viking ® and Easy-to-Read ® are registered trademarks of Penguin Group (USA) Inc.

Manufactured in China
Set in Bookman
Book design by Kelley McIntyre

To Michael, my hero
—D.C.

To Peter and David
—L.M.

Chapter One

Cork was a short muskrat.

He liked to play games.

He liked to win.

Fuzz was a tall possum.

He liked to play games.

He liked to win.

Two best friends.

Both liked to win.

"I want to have a race," Cork said.

"Me, too!" said Fuzz.

"I want to race down the hill," Cork said.

"Me, too!" said Fuzz.

"I want to win," Cork said.

"Me, too!" said Fuzz.

"No, no, no!" Cork said.

"You always win.

It is my turn to win!"

"We will see," said Fuzz.

"Ready! Set! Go!"

They raced down, down, down the hill.

Cork had short legs.

He ran *wump! wump! wump!*

Fuzz had longer legs.

He ran *zoom! zoom! zoom!*

Wump! Wump! Wump!

Zoom! Zoom! Zoom!

Wump! WHOOPS! Roll! Roll! Roll!

Cork rolled down the hill.

Fuzz ran *zoom! zoom! zoom!* to the

bottom of the hill.

"I win! I win!" Fuzz yelled.

Cork stopped rolling.

"No fair!" he said. "I tripped!

I fell! I rolled!"

"I won," Fuzz said.

"This is not a fun game," said Cork.

"I won," Fuzz said.

"I know you won!" Cork said. "You

do not have to keep telling me!"

"I won," Fuzz whispered.

Chapter Two

Cork picked up a long, fat stick.

"What are you doing with that stick?" Fuzz asked.

"I want to play stickball," Cork said.

"I do not know how to play stickball," Fuzz said.

"I will show you," Cork said.

He found a big, round pinecone.

"This pinecone will be the ball, right?"

"Right," said Fuzz. "And that stick will be the stick, right?"

"Right," said Cork.

"I am learning fast," Fuzz said.

"I will stand here," Cork said. "You throw the pinecone to me."

"Then what?" Fuzz asked.

"Then I will hit the pinecone," Cork said.

"I will run to that nut tree.

I will run to that big rock.

I will run to that thornbush.

Then I will run back here. I will win."

"When can I hold the stick?" asked Fuzz.

"After me," said Cork. "I thought of

the game. I get to hit first."

Fuzz threw the pinecone.

Cork swung the stick.

"You missed! My turn," Fuzz said.

Cork crawled under a bush to get

the pinecone.

Fuzz picked up the stick.

Cork threw the pinecone to Fuzz.

Fuzz whacked the pinecone with the stick.

The pinecone sailed over Cork's head.

Fuzz ran to the nut tree. *Zoom!*

He ran to the big rock. *Zoom!*

He ran to the thornbush. *Zoom!*

He ran back to Cork.

"I win! I win!" Fuzz yelled.

"No fair!" Cork said. "I was

supposed to win!"

"I won," Fuzz whispered.

"I do not like this game," Cork said.

"I want to play tackle ball.

It is my turn to win."

"We will see," said Fuzz.

Chapter Three

Cork found a long vine.

He wrapped the vine around and around

until it was as big as his head.

"This is the tackle ball," Cork said.

"It is not very round," Fuzz said. "It

looks like an egg ball."

"It is not an egg ball!" Cork said. "It is

a good tackle ball."

He handed the ball to Fuzz.

"You kick the ball," Cork said. "I will

catch it. I will run past those two apple

trees. That means I win."

"What do I do?" Fuzz asked.

"You try to tackle me," Cork said.

"But do not try too hard."

"We will see," said Fuzz.

Fuzz kicked the ball.

The ball went up, up, up into the air.

20

The ball came down, down, down
into Fuzz's arms.

Fuzz ran. *Zoom! Zoom! Zoom!*

"What are you doing?" Cork yelled.

"I am running to the apple trees!" Fuzz
yelled back. "Try to tackle me!"

Cork ran after Fuzz. *Wump! Wump! Wump!*

Cork could not tackle Fuzz.

"I win! I win!" Fuzz yelled.

"I am going home," Cork said. "I do not want to play anymore."

Cork walked away.

Fuzz sniffled.

Then he ran after Cork.

"Do not go!" Fuzz said. "Play one more
game. You will win this time!"

Cork stopped.

"Do you really think I will win?" he asked.

"We will see," said Fuzz.

Cork scratched his head, thinking.

Then he said, "I want to have a swim race."

Fuzz said, "But . . ."

"I want to race across the pond," Cork said.

Fuzz said, "But . . . but . . . but . . ."

"Ready! Set! Go!" yelled Cork.

Fuzz said, "But Cork, I do not know
how to swim!"

Chapter Four

Cork did not hear Fuzz.

He swam *swoosh! swoosh! swoosh!*

across the pond.

When he reached the other side,

he jumped out of the water.

"I win! I win!" he yelled. "Fuzz, I win!"

But Fuzz was not there.

"Fuzz?" Cork asked.

Cork swam back across the pond.

Fuzz was not in the water.

Fuzz was not on the pond bank.

Cork began to cry.

"My best friend has sunk!" he said.

He sat down on the pond bank.

He sat down on top of a wiggly thing.

"Snake!" Cork yelled.

He jumped up.

Cork looked at the wiggly thing again.

It was sticking out from under a bush.

It did not look like a snake at all.

It looked like a tail.

It looked like Fuzz's tail.

Cork pulled on it.

"Ow!" yelled Fuzz.

Cork pulled Fuzz out of the bush.

"You found me!" Fuzz yelled.

"You win!"

"But you did not swim," Cork said.

"I cannot swim," said Fuzz. "So I changed
the rules to hide-and-seek rules.
And you won!"

Cork put his arm around Fuzz's shoulders.

Fuzz put his arm around Cork's shoulders.

They laughed and ran down the hill.

Wump! Zoom! Wump! Zoom!

Two best friends, winners together.

"I do not care anymore if I win," Cork
said. "I thought my best friend was sunk.
I only care that you are still here."
Fuzz smiled. Then he said, "I know
a game that has two winners.
It is a three-legged race!"